Tundra Books, a division of Random House of Canada Limited, a Penguin Random House Company

LIBRARY AND ARCHIVES CANADA CATALOGUING IN PUBLICATION

Bar-el, Dan, author
    It's great being a Dad / Dan Bar-el ; illustrated by Gina Perry.
Issued in print and electronic formats.
ISBN 978-1-77049-605-7 (hardback).—ISBN 978-1-77049-607-1 (epub)
    I. Perry, Gina, 1976–, illustrator II. Title.
PS8553.A76229S69 2017   jC813'.54   C2016-900984-X
                                              C2016-900985-8

Published simultaneously in the United States of America by Tundra Books of Northern New York, a division of Random House of Canada Limited, a Penguin Random House Company

Library of Congress Control Number: 2016933061

Edited by Samantha Swenson
Designed by Five Seventeen
The artwork in this book was rendered in gouache and photoshop.
The text was set in Metro Nova Pro.
Printed and bound in China

www.penguinrandomhouse.ca

1 2 3 4 5   20 19 18 17 16

Penguin
Random
House

TUNDRA BOOKS

For Rose, who gave me the spark,
    and Randi, who gave me a chance
                    —DB

To my loves: Piper the Unicorn, Miles the Robot
    and Kristian the Dad
                    —GP

It's Great Being a Dad

by **Dan Bar-el**

illustrated by **Gina Perry**

TUNDRA BOOKS

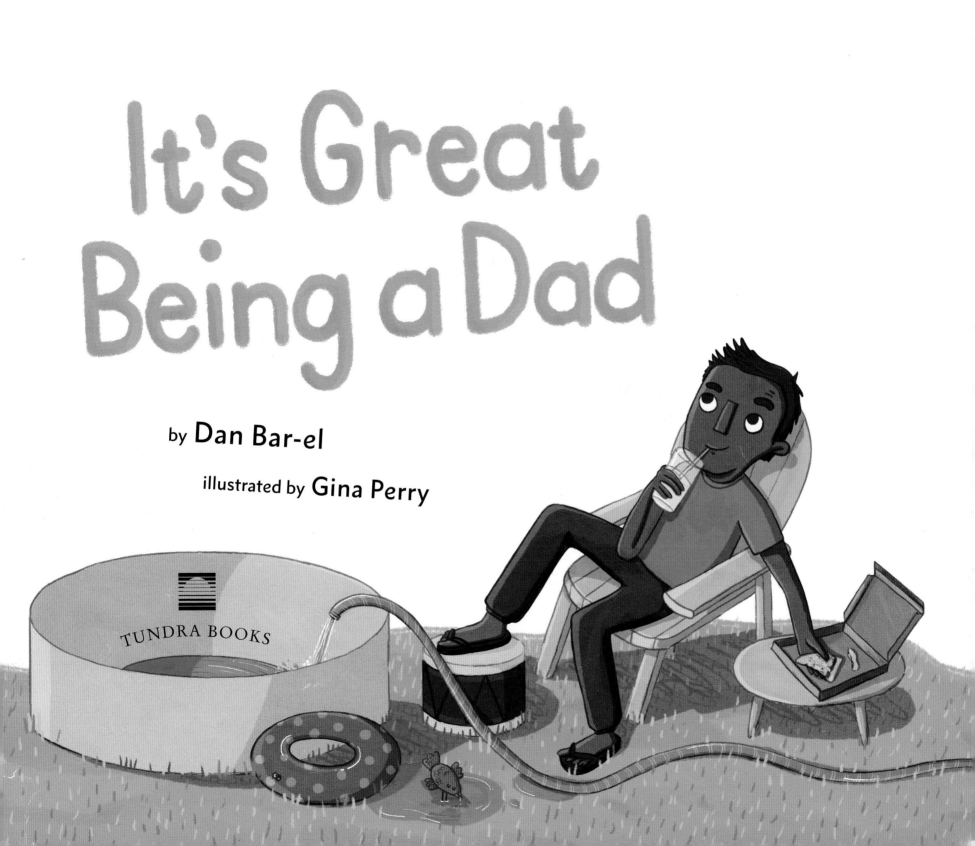

It's great being a unicorn. I love being a unicorn.
Who wouldn't want to be a unicorn?

We're terrific at prancing and we're very pretty
and, best of all, we have an adorable horn just above
our eyebrows.

So what's not to like about being a unicorn?

Grazing, that's what!

You try eating grass with a pointy thing sticking out of your forehead.
You go from the left, you go from the right; it's impossible.

And if you try to eat something tasty that's on a *table* . . .

. . . then you have a table stuck on your adorable horn!

It's great being Bigfoot. I love being Bigfoot. Who wouldn't want to be Bigfoot?

I'm covered in fur, so I'm never cold. I'm hard to find, so I get lots of privacy. And I'm super strong, so I can help unicorns get tables off their heads.

HELP!

So what's not to like about being Bigfoot?

Big feet, that's what!

There you are, trying to help a friend, and the next thing you know, you've put your big, strong foot right through a tree trunk.

It's great being a robot. If I had feelings, I would love being a robot. Who wouldn't want to be a robot?

I've got lots of flashing lights, so I'm easy to spot in the dark. I have lots of memory, so I never forget birthdays. And I have an arm that turns into a saw, so I can help unicorns and Bigfoot with their wood problems.

So what's not to like about being a robot?

Rain, that's what!

There you are, about to prove robots are superior, when suddenly your metal rusts and your hinges get stuck.

It's not so great being the Loch Ness Monster. I really don't like being the Loch Ness Monster. Who would want to be the Loch Ness Monster?

For one thing, I'm a monster. At least, that's what everyone says I'm supposed to be. I don't feel like a monster, but labels stick.

So what's to like about being the Loch Ness Monster?

It's great being a fairy queen ballerina doctor. I love being a fairy queen ballerina doctor. Who wouldn't want to be a fairy queen ballerina doctor?

HOSPITAL

If you're sick, I can give you medicine. If you're sad,
I can perform a happy dance.

If you have trouble with your saw arm . . .

. . . or your head horn or your big foot,
I can use my magic wand.

FWIP!

So what's not to like about being a
fairy queen ballerina doc—

Sneaky flying alligator pirates, that's what!
   Just when I'm about to save the day, he swoops
in and steals my magic wand! DAD!

It's great being a sneaky flying alligator pirate. I love being a sneaky flying alligator pirate. Who wouldn't want to be a sneaky flying alligator pirate?

I'm sneaky, so you never see me coming.

I can fly, so you can never catch me. And . . . And . . . that's enough reasons.

So what's not to like about being a sneaky flying alligator pirate?

BEEP!
BOOP!

Dads, that's what!

It's great being a dad. I love being a dad.

I get to remove tables from unicorns and tree stumps from Bigfoot.

I get to oil rusty saw arms and give awards to helpful monsters.

I get to return magic wands to . . . to . . .

"Fairy queen ballerina doctors. I told you a million times already."

Right. What she said.

Sudden makeovers, that's what!